# DANNY DODO'S
## DETECTIVE DIARY

### LEARN ALL ABOUT EXTINCT AND ENDANGERED ANIMALS

# HELLO, I'M DANNY DODO

I'm a detective on a mission. Over the years, hundreds of amazing animals have disappeared. Where did they go? What happened to them and why did they vanish from the Earth? It's my job to find out—and you can help!

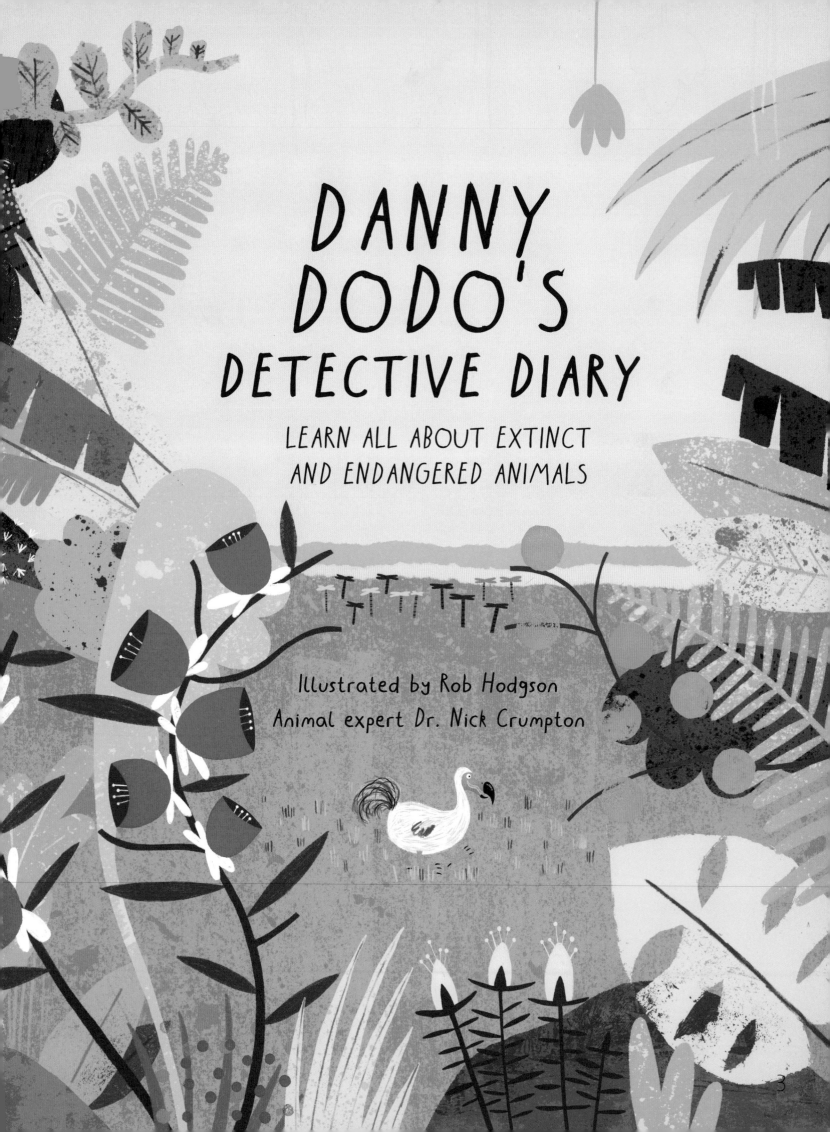

# DANNY DODO'S
## DETECTIVE DIARY

### LEARN ALL ABOUT EXTINCT
### AND ENDANGERED ANIMALS

Illustrated by Rob Hodgson

Animal expert Dr. Nick Crumpton

# CONTENTS

# A WORD OF WARNING

Did you know that there are thousands of endangered animal species all over the world? They are threatened in different ways. Some can't adapt quickly enough when their habitats start to change. Others find themselves competing with a stronger species. If we don't help them, they could become extinct, which means there won't be any of that type of animal left.

Some of these animals are in more trouble than others. They can be divided into three groups, based on how many of their kind are left.

## VULNERABLE

This means that the species is in danger from something that could make them extinct, such as hunting or habitat loss. Their problems are continuing or getting worse.

## ENDANGERED

Endangered species are almost extinct in the wild. There may be too few of them to find mates to keep the species alive. Sometimes, human beings capture these animals and help them to breed in captivity.

## EXTINCT

When an animal species becomes extinct, it vanishes from the world forever.

Extinction can make life harder for the species that are still alive. You see, lots of animal families are linked through the food chain, or because they share a habitat. That's why protecting the most endangered animals means that everyone has the best chance of survival.

Extinction isn't new, but things have got a lot worse since humans came along. Today, more than 26,500 species are in danger of extinction, and this number is getting higher every year. There are lots of reasons why this is happening.

## CLIMATE CHANGE

The Earth's atmosphere is getting warmer because of the things that humans do. This is called climate change. Forests are losing some of their plant species, and animals are dying out because they can't adapt to the hotter temperatures.

## LOSS OF HABITAT

Too much farming can damage the places where animals live. Livestock farming also produces lots of greenhouse gases, which make climate change worse.

## DEFORESTATION

Humans have cut down large numbers of trees around the world. This leads to climate change, the loss of clean water and the destruction of animal homes.

## OVER-HUNTING

Over the years, humans have hunted animals for food, for fur or even because they think it's fun. If too many animals are killed before the next generation can grow up, an entire species can be destroyed.

# DODO BIRD
## DETECTIVE DANNY

### MAURITIUS

You know me already! I don't like to blow my own horn, but I'm one of the most famous extinct animals. I was first seen by a human being in 1598, and I was last seen in 1662. I stood 3 ft tall, and with my high, bony head, my strong, hooked beak, and my jaunty tuft of tail feathers, I always turned heads. This is my story.

### GROUNDED

I used my wings for balancing and for display... but not for flying! Because I couldn't fly, I nested on the ground in the woods and near the coast. I was heavier than the birds who soared through the air, but I wasn't fat. I was the perfect size for me!

### MAURITIAN MEALS

My favorite foods were nuts, fruits, seeds and roots. With my powerful beak, I could eat very hard foods, and I was happy to share with the owls, pigeons, parakeets and herons that also lived here.

## HOW RUDE!

Now for something a bit upsetting. The sailors who visited Mauritius wanted to know what dodos tasted like! The answer? Not very nice, apparently. That didn't stop them from gobbling up several of my aunties, uncles and cousins.

## MYSTERY SOLVED

If you're thinking that we died out because humans ate too many of us, think again. We tasted yucky, remember? But the humans brought new animals with them—pigs and dogs, rats and cats—and they stole our food and our eggs. Meanwhile, the humans destroyed our habitat. It became too hard for us dodos to survive.

# DWARF ELEPHANTS
## SMALL PAUL

### THE MEDITERRANEAN

When big animals move to small islands, they often evolve to become smaller themselves. That's exactly what happened to Small Paul. Around 800,000 years ago, the sea level dropped and the 10-ton ancestors of the dwarf elephants started migrating onto islands across the Mediterranean, including Cyprus, Malta and Sicily. For a while, this life seemed to suit the dwarf elephants but in around 11,000 BCE they died out. Why?

### ISLAND LIFE

Small Paul's family found that food on the island was different from on the mainland and there was less of it. Over time their bodies evolved to be smaller, which meant they needed less to eat. By the time Small Paul was born, dwarf elephants weighed only 400 lb and were about 4.6 ft tall.

## ON THE MOVE

Just like the elephants, people were also spreading out and looking for new homes. They traveled across the Mediterranean and settled on Small Paul's island.

## MYSTERY SOLVED

Dwarf elephants were curious creatures and weren't afraid of humans. Sadly, this might have made them an easy target for hunters. Now there are no dwarf elephants left.

11

# SLOTH LEMURS
## DOUGLAS THE DUDE

### MADAGASCAR

Douglas the Dude was a laid-back sloth lemur who lived an easygoing life on the balmy beaches of Madagascar. He spent most of his time hanging out in the trees, grazing on vegan treats and chilling out with his friends. Which is why I'm so suspicious: how could an animal who was so calm and loveable—he's part-sloth, part-lemur for goodness' sake!—become extinct?

### SLOW SWINGER

Douglas the Dude was an Archaeoindris sloth lemur. These animals were about the size of a modern-day gorilla—much bigger than today's lemurs. Archaeoindris had short, wide skulls and spent most of their time on the ground, although Douglas also used his long arms to swing between the trees—very, very slowly.

### BENDY WENDY

One of Doug's best friends was called Wendy. She was a Palaeopropithecus, another type of sloth lemur. She had long arms and bendy joints, just like modern-day sloths, and was a total yoga addict. Her curved fingers worked like hooks, helping her to hang gracefully in mid-air. However, this also meant she was hopeless at walking on the ground.

## BUILT-IN BEAUTY

Douglas's glamorous Aunt Sophie was a medium-sized Babakotia sloth lemur. Instead of having normal teeth in her lower jaw, Aunt Sophie had a special row of them called a "toothcomb," which she used for grooming her fur—a built-in beauty accessory!

## HORRIFICALLY SLOW

Sloth lemurs lost their homes due to climate change and became extinct, but I have deduced that they were also hunted by humans. How do I know? Knife marks have been found on their bones—how horrible! They were just too heavy and too slow to move out of harm's way.

13

# STELLER'S SEA COW
## HUGE HOGARTH

### BERING SEA

Hogarth was a really, really big guy. Like everyone in his family, he grew up to 33 ft long—nearly the length of a bus. With his herd of females, infants and other males, this gentle giant moved slowly around his chilly home, harming no one. What made such a gargantuan guy disappear from the planet?

### SUPER SEAFOOD

Hogarth didn't have any teeth, but that didn't stop him from enjoying a meal of seagrass and seaweed. He used the bony pads in his mouth to grind up his food.

## GRUESOME SAILORS

In 1741, some Russian sailors were marooned on an island. They spotted Hogarth's herd and soon found that the sea cows were easy to hunt. Their meat tasted good and more humans arrived to try it for themselves. In just 27 years, all Steller's sea cows were hunted to extinction.

## HAPPY HERDS

Hogarth loved spending time with his herd in cool, shallow water where he could use his stubby forelimbs to push himself along on the ground, just like you might push yourself along on a scooter!

15

# GREAT AUK
## SUKI THE SWIMMING STAR
### ARCTIC OCEAN

Talented Suki was no ordinary bird—
she used her stubby wings to glide
underwater instead of flying through
the air. She loved the water so much,
she roosted as close to it as possible.
I've discovered that Suki was hunted by
human beings—but why?

## PEACEFUL PERSONALITY
Chilled-out Suki and her
friends were gentle birds with
no way to defend themselves.

## WATER WINGS

Suki's striking looks made her easy to spot in the Arctic Ocean. At 2.5 ft tall, with a large, grooved, black beak, she was very hard to miss, especially when she stood up.

## HUNTED DOWN

Great auks like Suki were killed in huge numbers. What did humans want from them? The answer is "everything:" their meat, their fat and their feathers. As they became rarer, their eggs grew more valuable to collectors.

17

# PARROTS

Like me, many of these awesome birds have disappeared from the modern world. 28 percent of all parrot species are listed as "globally threatened" because of poaching and habitat loss. But there's some good news! Humans who care about animals are now working hard to put things right.

## CUBAN MACAW
### EXTRAORDINARY EVA, CUBA

This small and colorful supermodel lived with her family. Her beauty was admired by humans, who captured her and sold her as a pet. The same thing happened to many other members of her family and their habitat began to suffer too. When hurricanes hit Cuba year after year, the number of macaws dropped even further.

## CAROLINA PARAKEET
### HANK THE HIPSTER, UNITED STATES

With his green, red, orange and yellow feathers, Hank was always dressed for a party. He was one of a flock of 200 and everyone knew him. But their habitat was limited and when humans started to cut down the forests, the parakeets were in trouble.

## SPIX'S MACAW
### BASHFUL ANA, BRAZIL

For shy, family-loving macaws like Ana, home sweet home used to be in the driest parts of Brazil, close to the rivers. They nested in big Carabeira trees and Ana used the same one every year. When humans started cutting down the trees, the macaws' homes were quickly destroyed.

## FUTURE HOPE

After the pet trade, habitat loss and hurricanes, the last Cuban macaws died off around 1865. Deforestation, hunting and disease destroyed Hank's family of Carolina parakeets in the early 1900s. But I've discovered some good news about Ana and her folks! Even though Spix's macaws are extinct in the wild, they are being bred in captivity. Hopefully, humans will stop these beautiful birds from disappearing.

19

# TASMANIAN TIGER
## LADY TASHA

### AUSTRALASIA

Elegant Lady Tasha was an inquisitive hunter who would have made a splendid detective—and I should know! Her family was powerful, determined and secretive. Even though the tigers died out on the Australian mainland 3,000 years ago, thousands of them survived on an island called Tasmania. Tasha was very clever and she had the best memory on the island.

### BIG BITE

Tasha had strong jaws that could open incredibly wide, so she could get a really good grip on her prey. Her naughty Uncle Max hunted farm animals like sheep and chickens, which turned farmers against the whole family. Hey, he was just trying to stay alive!

## NO ESCAPE

As well as her great strength, Tasha had a lot of stamina. That meant that she could chase her prey for a very long time, until it was too exhausted to run any more.

## HOME SWEET HOME

Tasha's shelter was called a lair. Like everyone in her family, she had more than one home—some in caves, some under rocks—because she hunted across such a wide area. She liked her home comforts, and always made sure that there were soft leaves and grass to lie on.

## TROUBLE FOR TASHA

In the 1800s, Europeans invaded Australia and the islands around it, and settled there permanently. Farmers shot at Tasha if they saw her near their livestock. Her habitat changed and she had to battle new animals and diseases. The last known Tasmanian tiger in the wild died in 1930. Just 6 years later, the last one in captivity died too.

21

# BAIJI
## MADAM MAYLEEN

### CHINA

Short-sighted Madam Mayleen was a baiji, but people also called her the Yangtze River dolphin and made up wild stories about her. They believed that dolphins had magical powers and eating their meat would give protection from evil spirits. I investigated this because I didn't believe she really had superpowers but I fell under her spell! Everyone agreed that Madam Mayleen was special.

### SUPER SONAR

Mayleen's eyesight wasn't great, but that was OK—she didn't need it! The Yangtze River was so dark that good eyesight would have been useless. Instead she used sound to find her way around.

## UNFORGETTABLE

At 8 ft long, Mayleen was a little bigger than the males of her kind and she charmed them all with her bubbly personality.

## MODERN LIFE

So why did Madam Mayleen disappear from the river? Baiji like her had lived there for 20 million years. Over time, people started to use the river in different ways. There was more transport and fishing, and hydroelectric dams were built. Industrial waste polluted the water and humans invaded their habitat. It was impossible for the baiji to survive.

# WESTERN BLACK RHINO
## PROUD PERCY
### AFRICA

Like all black rhinos, Percy loved his mom. He stayed with her for 3 years before setting off to make his way in the world. When he was very young, lions tried to catch him and he couldn't wait to grow too big for them to attack. His first horn was more than 3 ft long and Percy was very proud of it!

## THE GOOD OLD DAYS

Before they disappeared, western black rhinos were around for more than 7 million years, roaming across countries including South Sudan, Cameroon and Niger.

24

## HARD TIMES

In the early 20th century, life grew difficult for Percy and his friends. People started hunting the rhinos for sport or to stop them from eating their crops. At the same time more industrial farms were built, destroying the rhinos' habitat.

## MEDICAL PROBLEMS

In the mid-20th century, traditional Chinese medicine became popular in Asia. Some people believed that ground-up rhino's horn had healing powers, so the animals were hunted and killed. Rhino horn was also used to make knife handles. By 2011, the western black rhino was extinct.

## HELPFUL HUMANS

Even though Percy and his family have gone, there are still some black rhinos left. With the help of kind human beings, the eastern black, the south-central and the south-western rhinos can still survive. And my detective instinct tells me that there are still some animal-loving people out there who care!

# FROGS AND TOADS

These quiet animals spent most of their time avoiding humans, so how did such private creatures end up extinct? I suspected that there was more to their stories...

## GASTRIC BROODING FROG
### GERTIE THE GOBBLER, EAST AUSTRALIA

Gertie and her folks loved the water and never lived far from a river or stream. They made their homes in forests and the whole family stayed close together. I couldn't believe it when I found out how she kept her babies safe. Gertie swallowed her eggs! By the time she spat them back out, they were fully developed frogs. Clever stuff ... but I'm glad my mom didn't try it!

## GOLDEN TOAD
### AWESOME ANGELO, COSTA RICA

Angelo was a handsome fellow who loved bright colors. He lived in a tiny corner of a cloud forest and wouldn't set one webbed foot out of his underground burrow until he was looking his best. He hasn't been seen for over 30 years.

## SRI LANKAN SHRUB FROG
### SCATTER-BRAINED LOLA, SRI LANKA

Lola was so keen to grow up that she skipped the tadpole phase and went straight from being a tiny egg to becoming a little frog. That meant that she didn't need much water, so she could live wherever she chose as long as it was damp. She was a hopeless mom though —she laid her eggs among fallen leaves and then left them to fend for themselves!

## RABBS' FRINGE-LIMBED FROG
### AIR FORCE FINN, PANAMA

Everyone in Panama was talking about the amazing flying frog, so I checked him out! Finn lived high up in the cloud forest and used his huge, webbed feet to glide through the air. It was a great way to escape from predators! He was a good dad, but a clueless cook. He fed his babies on bits of old skin from his back!

## USUAL SUSPECTS

Four well-known troublemakers kept coming up during my investigations—humans, disease, habitat loss and climate change. Gertie, Angelo, Finn and Lola all suffered because of this fearsome four.

27

# PASSENGER PIGEON
## SKYE THE SIGHTSEER

### USA

Skye was a restless traveler who loved to look on-trend. She never settled in one deciduous forest because the next one was always calling! There was so much of the world that she wanted to see, and she never went anywhere without her long, white-fringed tail—her favorite fashion accessory.

### SUPER SPEED

Skye was an extremely fast flyer. She could reach 96 km per hour thanks to her slim body shape and powerful muscles, which helped her to cut through the air.

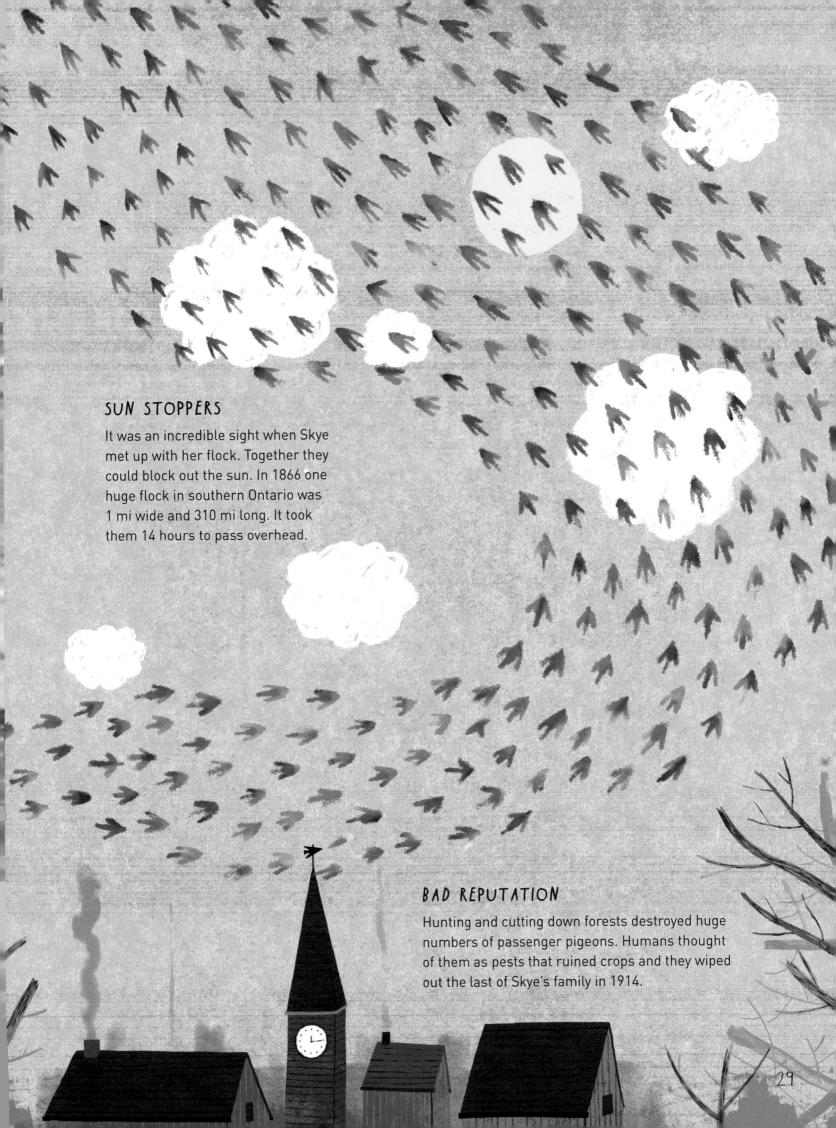

## SUN STOPPERS

It was an incredible sight when Skye
met up with her flock. Together they
could block out the sun. In 1866 one
huge flock in southern Ontario was
1 mi wide and 310 mi long. It took
them 14 hours to pass overhead.

## BAD REPUTATION

Hunting and cutting down forests destroyed huge
numbers of passenger pigeons. Humans thought
of them as pests that ruined crops and they wiped
out the last of Skye's family in 1914.

# TREE SNAIL
## LILY THE LEGEND

### HAWAII

The islands of Hawaii are known for their music and dancing, and Lily the tree snail had all the coolest and slowest hula moves. She shared her home with over 750 snail species, including more than 200 types of tree snail. But since the year 1500 nearly half of all the animals that have become extinct have been land snails and slugs. How could such dazzling dancers just disappear?

### POETS' MUSE

Lily was less than one inch but she was so colorful and shiny that humans made up stories about her. Some of them even wrote poems!

## SPECIAL SPIRAL

Most snail shells spiral to the right, but Lily liked to do things differently—her shell coiled to the left!

## HEALTHY EATING

Lily kept herself in shape by dining on yummy fungus that grew on plants.

## ANIMAL ENEMIES

The humans who came to the islands brought animals including deer, goats and pigs, which destroyed snail habitats. They also brought hungry rats and chameleons. Even more awful was Lily's archenemy, the dreaded rosy wolf snail, who actually ate other snails!

# PINTA ISLAND TORTOISE
## GORDON THE GARDENER

### GALÁPAGOS ISLANDS

Gordon and his gardening gang first arrived on the Galápagos Islands 5 million years ago. They rode in the strong ocean currents all the way from South America, searching for a new place to call home. What happened to these slow-moving animals who worked to help the planet?

### STICKING HIS NECK OUT

Gordon settled on Pinta where he found grass and fruit to eat. His long neck helped him to survive the dry hot season—he could stretch it to reach food such as the prickly pear cactus.

## CARETAKERS

The tortoises kept the Galápagos Islands tidy in the 1800s. But when goats were brought to Pinta Island in the 20th century, they damaged the habitat so badly that the tortoises could not find enough food to survive.

## EXCITING NEWS

You can't keep a good tortoise down. In 2019, a female Fernandina giant tortoise was found in the Galápagos National Park—110 years since the last one had been seen in the wild. She is probably over 100 years old. Even better, there may be more giant tortoises in hiding, because there were other footprints and dung (or poop!) nearby. Maybe the gardening tortoises will soon be back again!

# MOA
## MIGHTY MILLICENT

### NEW ZEALAND

When I was questioning witnesses, I found that lots of the locals were scared of Millicent the upland moa. There were 9 species of moa, a type of flightless bird, and Millicent and her kind were one of the largest, growing to almost 10 ft tall. Twice as heavy as the males of her species, Millicent was quite a formidable figure!

### LOUD AND PROUD

Even the enormous Haast's eagle, which liked to hunt moas, stayed away from Millicent! Her deep, booming voice sent everyone running.

### LEG WARMERS

Millicent liked to live high up in the mountains where it could get pretty chilly. She was very proud of her natural feathered leg warmers, which kept her nice and toasty.

## MEAT-FREE DIET

Millicent was a vegetarian, and her favorite foods were seeds, grass and leaves. She couldn't fly but she walked with her head held high.

## CLUE TO EXTINCTION

Why did so many birds become extinct in less than 100 years? When humans arrived in New Zealand, they hunted the moa for its meat and used its bones to make fishhooks and needles.

35

# BUCARDO
## BILLY THE BALLET STAR

### PYRENEES, FRANCE AND SPAIN

One of my most fascinating cases involved Billy, a fierce-looking Pyrenean bucardo. His horns were 3 ft long and he weighed 220 lb. Everyone told me that he was scary. But he was very nimble and I found out that he was actually a talented parkour star!

### HOME STONY HOME

Billy liked leaping around in rocky places like cliffs, where he could graze on herbs, lichen and grass. A sociable goat, he could often be found visiting friends who lived on tough patches of farmland and on the rocky coast.

## NO FROZEN DINNERS!

As the weather changed Billy and his family made sure they could find food by moving up and down the mountain, staying on thawed ground.

## TOO MUCH COMPETITION

Humans brought other grazing animals to the area like deer, sheep and goats. Soon there were too many animals and not enough food. Billy's free-running days were soon over.

# GUAM KINGFISHER
## CRANKY KITTY

### GUAM, MICRONESIA

The island of Guam was once home to a noisy, grumpy bird called Kitty. It wasn't hard to investigate her—everyone said she was hard to forget. She was only 8 in long but if anyone dared to cross her land she made a very BIG fuss in her chattering, raspy voice.

### SMASH AND NEST

Kitty wasn't a dainty homemaker. She smashed tree bark with her big, strong beak to make her nest.

### TASTY TREATS

Some kingfishers need to live near water, but not Kitty. She made her home inland, snapping up small lizards and insects from the ground and grumbling at anyone who got in her way.

## SNAKES IN THE GRASS

Guam kingfishers like Kitty disappeared from the wild over 30 years ago and I followed the clues to find out why. In the 1940s, humans accidentally brought snakes to the island and those greedy reptiles gobbled up the kingfishers' eggs. Now there are no kingfishers left on the island, but there are around 2 million brown tree snakes.

## HOPE FOR THE FUTURE

There's a happy ending for Kitty's relatives. Conservationists managed to capture 20 Guam kingfishers and their chicks have been hand-reared in zoos. There aren't many of them left in the world, but their chances are looking up.

39

# ENDANGERED ANIMALS
## ON LAND

My mission is almost complete! We've learned about a lot of amazing animals and we've solved plenty of mysteries along the way. But I'm hoping that we won't have any more extinct animals to investigate. All good detectives know that it's better to stop a crime before it happens. Right now, there are thousands of species in danger of disappearing. With your help, maybe we can keep them safe!

## SHRILL CARDER BEE

This little bumblebee builds its nest in the ground. The number of carder bees in the U.K. has fallen because so many flower-filled meadows have been lost.

## AMUR LEOPARD

The biggest threats to this rare leopard are poaching and loss of habitat. There are only about 100 Amur leopards left on the border between Russia and China. It's a chilly spot, so the leopards grow thick fur to keep cozy.

## SUNDA PANGOLIN

These scaly anteaters live in the trees of southeast Asia. They are in danger because people eat them and use their scales to make medicine. The pangolins try to protect themselves by curling up into a ball but that makes them easier for humans to pick up.

## TAPANULI ORANGUTAN

These fruit-loving great apes live in the trees on the Indonesian island of Sumatra. There are fewer than 800 left because their home is being destroyed. Humans are cutting down the trees to make room for a dam that will provide water and electricity.

## AXOLOTL

These Mexican amphibians have a superpower: if they are injured, they can grow new body parts! They have few predators, but are endangered due to pollution and poaching, and because humans build on the lakes and ponds where they live.

41

# ENDANGERED ANIMALS
## IN THE SEA

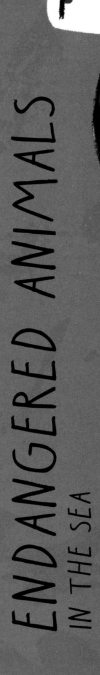

### SHY ALBATROSS

Global warming and pollution threaten to destroy these large Australian seabirds. They mate for life and lay just one precious egg every year.

### SOUTHERN BLUEFIN TUNA

These speedy swimmers are at risk because they are hunted by humans for food. When they're left alone, they can live for up to 40 years and grow up to 8 ft long. They are found across the oceans of the Southern Hemisphere in open water.

### VAQUITA

There are only 10–15 of these shy little porpoises left in the world. They get caught in fishing nets by accident, so scientists are working hard to remove any abandoned nets that the porpoises might get tangled in.

## HUMPHEAD WRASSE

At over 6.5 ft long, this fish is easy to spot on the reefs of the Coral Triangle in the Pacific Ocean. Because it is seen as a luxury food it can earn poachers a lot of money. Their fishing methods have put the whole species at risk.

## ORNATE EAGLE RAY

At home in the Indian Ocean, these playful rays love leaping out of the water. They can grow to be 8 ft wide. Unfortunately they often get caught accidentally by fishing boats.

# WHAT CAN YOU DO?

Plenty! There are lots of ways that you can help the animals who share our planet.

## PROBLEM: INTENSIVE FARMING

### SOLUTION: EAT MORE VEGGIES

Farming large numbers of animals for meat and dairy products can be damaging to the land and to the other animals living on it. If we eat less meat, farmers won't need to use so much land.

## PROBLEM: LOSS OF TREES

### SOLUTION: CHOOSE FSC PAPER

When you buy something made of paper or wood, check that it has been grown in a sustainable way and is approved by the Forest Stewardship Council.

## PROBLEM: POLLUTION

### SOLUTION: REDUCE, REUSE, RECYCLE

Humans keep throwing away plastic, which takes hundreds of years to break down. It affects the land, ocean and animals, so try to use less plastic and recycle and reuse everything that you can. And of course, don't be a litter bug!

## PROBLEM: CLIMATE CHANGE

### SOLUTION: USE CLEANER TRANSIT

Cars and planes produce a lot of air pollution. Try traveling by train or bicycle where you can. If you have to travel by car, why not try to organize a school-day carpool (with your parents' help).

## PROBLEM: HABITAT LOSS

### SOLUTION: GET INTO GARDENING!

Cities have been built over many animals' habitats. You can help by putting up bird boxes and suet cakes, building an insect hotel, planting bee-friendly blooms or adding hedgehog-sized holes to the bottom of your garden fence.

## PROBLEM: LOSS OF WATER

### SOLUTION: USE LESS WATER

Rivers, lakes and wetlands are under a lot of pressure to provide water for humans. The amount of freshwater wildlife has gone down by 83 percent since 1970. You can help to protect freshwater ecosystems by using less water.

## PROBLEM: ADULTS AREN'T LISTENING

SAVE THE WHALES

I'M A BIG FAN OF RENEWABLE ENERGY

EAT GREEN

PEDAL POWER

DANNY DODO'S

THERE IS NO PLANET B!

### SOLUTION: FIND YOUR VOICE!

You can make a difference by telling adults you know about the animals in this book. Explain what happened to us and tell them how to help animals around the world!

# GLOSSARY

Here's all the lingo that you need to know to sound like an animal expert.

ANCESTOR – an early animal or plant from which a later species has evolved.

CAPTIVITY – when animals live under human care in farms and zoos.

CARNIVORE – any creature that eats mostly meat.

CLOUD FOREST – a tropical forest with low-level cloud cover.

CONSERVATIONIST – a person who protects and preserves the environment and wildlife.

DEFORESTATION – when humans cut down and clear forests.

DESCENDANT – an animal or person related to someone from an earlier generation.

DIGESTION – when your body breaks down food so you can use it for energy. This is how we get vitamins and nutrients.

ENDANGERED – a species that is likely to become extinct in the future because there are very few animals left in the wild.

EVOLVE – when the body parts of an animal or plant slowly change over time.

EXTINCT – an animal is extinct when no members of its species are left alive.

GLOBAL WARMING – the process of rising temperatures on our planet over time.

GREENHOUSE GASES – gases in the Earth's atmosphere (like carbon dioxide) that trap energy from the sun.

HERBIVORE – an animal that eats only plants.

HERD – a large group of animals. They live and feed together.

MIGRATE – when animals move from one region or habitat, usually once a year.

POACHING – to illegally hunt animals.

PREDATOR – an animal that hunts and kills other animals for food.

PREY – an animal that is hunted or caught by other animals.

REPTILE – a cold-blooded animal that is covered in scales or plates, and lays eggs.

VULNERABLE – a species that is likely to become endangered due to declining numbers in the wild.

# INDEX

First published in the United States of America in 2021 by
Thames & Hudson Inc., 500 Fifth Avenue, New York, New York 10110

*Danny Dodo's Detective Diary* © 2021 Thames & Hudson Ltd, London
Illustrations © 2021 Rob Hodgson

Text by Rachel Elliot
Designed by Emily Sear
Consultancy by Dr. Nick Crumpton

Library of Congress Control Number 2020944702

ISBN 978-0-500-65207-7

Printed and bound in China by C & C Offset Printing Co. Ltd

MIX
Paper from
responsible sources
FSC® C008047
FSC
www.fsc.org

Be the first to know about our new releases,
exclusive content and author events by visiting
**thamesandhudson.com**
**thamesandhudsonusa.com**
**thamesandhudson.com.au**